10/07x1
10/09x5

MAR 1 5 2004

Rabén & Sjögren Bokförlag, Stockholm
www.raben.se

Translation copyright © 2003 by Elisabeth Kallick Dyssegaard
All rights reserved
Originally published in Sweden by Rabén & Sjögren under the
title *Bertil och Badrums-Elefanterna*
Text copyright © 2002 by Inger Lindahl
Pictures copyright © 2002 by Eva Lindström
Library of Congress Control Number: 2002114528
Printed in Denmark
First American edition, 2003
ISBN 91-29-65944-2

INGER LINDAHL   EVA LINDSTRÖM

BERTIL
and the
Bathroom
Elephants

Translated by
Elisabeth Kallick Dyssegaard

R&S
BOOKS

Stockholm   New York   London   Adelaide   Toronto

Bertil is just three years old, but he's already really good at throwing and banging.

You could say he's a little wild. And he splashes! When he takes a bath, he sprays whole oceans on the floor.

"Bertil! My socks are getting soaked!" shouts Mom.
She doesn't like a bathroom sea. As if that's Bertil's fault!
As if everything in the whole world is Bertil's fault! In fact,
it's not. At least, not the flooding.
"It's the elephants!"
"The what?" says Mom.

"That's right. Bathroom elephants. A pair of them. They live there," Bertil says, pointing under the tub. "They spray a lot."

Bertil fills his cheeks with water. *Pop.* He slaps his cheeks, and a fountain spurts out of his mouth.

"They squirt with their trunks even though I've told them not to," he says, sounding upset.

"I see. Then I have to scold the elephants, not you," says Mom. She bends down and looks under the tub.

"Stop that, you bad elephants!" she shouts. "You'll have to quit spraying if you are going to live here!"

The elephants try to stop. They'd really like to live here.
But they keep on acting wild. It's not so easy to quit.
At the dinner table, Bertil talks about their pranks. And
everyone laughs.

Mom, Dad, and Bertil's big brother, Ziggy—everyone laughs.

One day the toilet is clogged up. Completely! You can't flush it anymore. The water reaches all the way to the top of the bowl. Dad gets the toolbox.

"Does anyone know how this happened?" asks Mom.

Ziggy looks at Bertil. Bertil looks at a crack in the ceiling.

"Well?" says Mom. She doesn't look happy.

"I told them not to, but they did it anyway," says Bertil quietly.

"Did what?"

"Flushed Dad's underwear," he whispers.

"That's it!" says Mom. She is really mad.

Suddenly Dad gets a bite! There's a sucking sound in the toilet, and the water level goes down. On his finger hangs a pair of wet underwear with green fish.

"Yuck! These really are awful," says Dad and wrinkles his nose.

He's right. Everyone laughs, and the bathroom elephants get to stay.

"Pay attention! I'm giving you names!"
Bertil tells the elephants, turning the
water on full force.

He calls them Ray and Spray. He's
good at naming bathroom elephants! He
can hear them giggling under the tub.

"They like me," says Bertil proudly.
"They probably think I'm their dad."

Bertil knows what the bathroom elephants need:
raisins. Lots of raisins. They are extremely hungry.

Mom thinks one plate of raisins a day will be
enough. She puts it out in the bathroom in the
evening. In the morning the plate is empty.

"How strange that they eat raisins," says Ziggy.
"I've never heard that about elephants."

"Ordinary elephants, no. But bathroom
elephants are different," Bertil says and burps.

One day when Bertil is sitting on the toilet, thinking out loud about this and that, he hears the elephants growl at him. Not giggle, but growl!

Grrr, grrrrrr . . . grrr: a deep, hoarse sound from under the tub. It is very disturbing. Bertil can't think his thoughts in peace and quiet any longer. Are the elephants mad at him? Or just hungry? He asks Mom to put some extra raisins on the plate that evening. But the elephants continue to growl.

GRRR, GRRR, GRRR . . .

"Be quiet!" Bertil finally shouts.

He shouldn't have done that. Quick as lightning, the elephants stick out their trunks and try to catch him by the legs.

"HELP!"

Now Mom has to come with Bertil to the bathroom.

"They are lying there waiting," whispers Bertil, pointing at the tub. "If you leave, they'll grab me by the feet."

Mom shines a flashlight under the tub.

"There are no elephants there," she says.

Bertil doesn't believe her.

"Stay right here! Don't leave me," he hisses.

That's when Mom stops feeding the elephants.

"If they don't get any food, they'll die of hunger," she says.

Three weeks pass. Not one little raisin! She looks under the tub. Completely empty of bathroom elephants.

"Gone! They've probably moved."

Bertil looks, too. He doesn't see any elephants. Finally he dares to believe it's true. They're really gone!

Bertil's no longer afraid to go to the bathroom by himself. Those elephants were kind of dumb, he thinks. It's wonderful to be rid of them.
    "Bang!"

The hand-towel hook comes loose and falls to the floor with a crash.

"Help, the elephants are killing me! Help!"

Bertil tries to escape into the hallway, but he can't run with his pants down around his ankles.

"Calm down!" says Mom. "It was probably just a little damp behind the towel hook."

"They tried to kill me!" screams Bertil. "I'm never going in there again. Never!"

The potty has to be brought down from the attic. Bertil sits on the potty in the hallway and stares anxiously at the bathroom door. No more peace and quiet!

He doesn't talk about the elephants anymore.

Never again!

Time passes—days, weeks . . .

"Pest-Be-Gone!" Ziggy suddenly remembers.

"What?"

"Call Pest-Be-Gone. They'll come and spray away the elephants."

How clever Ziggy is! He knows so much, and he's only six years old.

"That's what we'll do," says Dad enthusiastically. "What are we waiting for?"

And while Bertil and Ziggy are at school, the Pest-Be-Gone men come. They spray under the tub, and through the entire apartment.

"You'll never see those elephants again," the Pest-Be-Gone men promise as they leave.

That night Bertil has nightmares. Angry elephants chase him around the apartment. He screams and wakes up the whole family. He's so scared that he gets to sleep between Mom and Dad.

In the morning he scolds his parents.

"You see. The elephants are still here. Just my luck. Now they are even angrier at me."

"But, sweetie, you were just dreaming. It was a dream," says Mom.

"A dream! Ha! Don't try to tell me that!" says Bertil, folding his arms across his chest.

What is Bertil going to do now? Nothing seems to help. Will he have to use a potty in the hallway for the rest of his life?

One day there's a knock at the door. It's Steven, their neighbor.

"Excuse me. I didn't mean to disturb you in the middle of dinner," he says. "But I was wondering if by any chance you had any bathroom elephants."

Everyone looks at him, mouths open in surprise. Everyone except Dad.

"Yes, we had a bad pair," says Dad. "But they are gone now. Either they died when Pest-Be-Gone sprayed or they moved out."

"I think that they have moved in with me," says Steven, looking guilty. "I love this kind of elephant. Bengali bathroom elephants."

Bertil just gapes. For once he's completely silent. Mom is, too. She stares at Steven.

"They just came marching in one day when I was playing my saxophone. I wasn't planning to steal them," Steven assures them.

"Of course not," says Dad. "Elephants love the saxophone. I had forgotten. But that's good, because they'll be happy with you. We'd be pleased if you kept them."

"Then it's okay if I keep the elephants?" asks Steven hopefully.

"Yes, it's fine with me," says Dad. "What do you think, Bertil?"

Bertil nods, and Steven leaves.

"What a nice guy Steven is!" says Dad. "And he knows about engines. He's the one who helped me with the car yesterday. Really great guy! And how lucky it is that Bengali bathroom elephants like the saxophone!"

After dinner Bertil goes to the bathroom. He sits there in peace and quiet and talks to himself for a long, long time. Then he shouts:
"DONE!"